USBORNE

Write and Draw your own Comics

Write and Draw your own Comics

With amazing comic strips by...

Dylan Marand

Write your name up there.

Contents

How to use this book   6

Comics: the basics   8

Making up characters   10

Drawing characters   12

Action drawings   14

Speech bubbles   16

Sound effects   18

Once upon a blank   20

Plotting   24

Rough planning   26

Pencils and inks   28

Your own comics   30

What shall I make a comic about today?

KAPOW!

Mix and match comic   32

Good day, bad day   38

Superheroes vs robots   44

Dinos in danger   50

Pirates and treasure   56

Tiny adventure   62

Secret agents   68

Fantasy quest   74

How to be a cat   80

Time travel   86

Drawing covers   92

A few last tips   94

Make a comic about me!

No, about me! I'm fascinating!

How to use this book

Comics use words and pictures to tell stories. This book has lots of space for you to write and draw your own comic strips, but there are also strips that have been drawn already to guide you.

There are lots of comic strips explaining important comics-making techniques.

Early in the book you'll find simple writing and drawing activities.

Later in the book you'll find comic strips giving you ideas for stories.

Your title goes here.

Your comics go here.

There are lots of tips around the edges of the pages.

At the end of the book there are stickers to use in your comics, too.

Stickers

Useful things

Pencils

A sharpener

A ruler

An eraser

RUB RUB

Pens, especially fine black pens, for drawing outlines

Spare paper for sketching out ideas for your comics

A dictionary and a thesaurus might come in handy.

What's another word for "big"? Big explosion doesn't sound dramatic enough.

Comics to read for inspiration

You can explore comics websites, too, using the Usborne Quicklinks website (see page 96).

Thesaurus

DICTIONARY

Comics: the basics

9

Making up characters

Your character

Turn this stick figure into a character by adding clothes and accessories. Fill in the blanks in the thought and speech bubbles, too.

Hello, my name is
Dreg
and the thing *I* want most in life is
Kill .

One thing no one knows about me is...
were I
Cour pram .

Giving your character a distinctive feature or two means your reader can easily tell that it's the same person all the way through your comic.

Ideas for features and accessories

Drawing characters

In comics, you can draw faces in all sorts of different ways.

Here are a few ways to draw parts of faces.

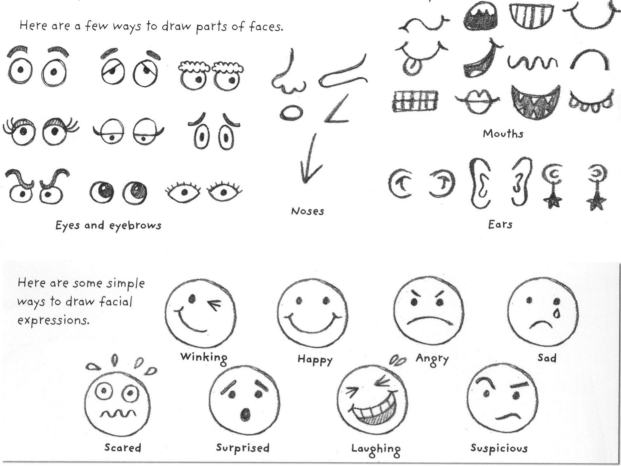

Eyes and eyebrows

Noses

Mouths

Ears

Here are some simple ways to draw facial expressions.

Winking   Happy   Angry   Sad

Scared   Surprised   Laughing   Suspicious

Now try adding expressions and features to these faces to match their names.

Suzy Brightside   Rocky Hardnut   Baddie McNasty   General Temperburst

Characters come in all shapes and sizes.
Here are a few basic body types you can use in your comics.

You could start with a stick figure and build up from there.

You could start with a rectangle or square to build up a stocky character.

For a toddler character, make it three times the height of its own head.

One head height

Grown-up human

Stocky monster

Ninja toddler

Draw your own characters with different body types. Add some details and facial expressions.

Name: ....

Name: ....

Name: ....

Action drawings

When you're making up characters, try drawing them in lots of different action poses. That helps you get a better feel for how they move around the page.

The little lines next to the figures show movement.

Some action poses to try in your comics

Shrugging

Running

Falling

Cowering in fear

Kicking a ball

SCRAMBLE!

Clinging to a cliff

Climbing

"I have a sore back" pose

Trying to pick up something heavy

100

Walking

Dancing

Slouching along sadly

Swimming

You can spread actions over several panels.
For example, here is a character jumping over an abyss.

Here are some four-legged creatures in action.

Dragon

Flying

Dog

Running

Cow

Oops, fallen over

Try drawing a four-legged creature in action.

Drawing animals doing human activities can be funny.

Speech bubbles

Comics use speech bubbles — also known as speech balloons —
to show that a character is talking.

It's usually easier to draw your pictures first, leaving room for speech bubbles.

Room for a speech bubble.

Write what your character says in pencil first...

I am a sneaky ninja.

...then draw a bubble around the words, with a "stem" pointing to the speaker.

Stem

I am a sneaky ninja.

Finally, go over the words and bubble in ink and erase the pencil lines.

I am a sneaky ninja.

Here are a few different types of speech bubble to use in your comics.

I'm whispering.

If your character has a lot to say you can use linked bubbles.

This means you don't have to have a huge chunk of writing all at once.

I'm shouting!

This is a thought bubble.

What do you think these animals are saying?
Add *speech bubbles* to show their conversation.

Sound effects

Noises in comics are sometimes called sound effects or SFX. The letter shapes used for SFX often reflect the sounds that are being made.

Escaping gas

Pffffft

Something disappearing

POUF !

Bigger, bolder letters make the sound seem louder.

Really loud explosion

KABOOM!

You can draw your SFX inside shapes to make them stand out more.

DING DONG!

SPLAT

This lion's roar is drawn in rough, hairy letters.

ROAAAAR!

EEEK!

Wooooo

BAM!

CRASH

Try making up your own words to describe noises.

FWEEEP!

MOO!

POW

School trip of terror

Use the stickers at the end of this book to add sound effects to this comic.

Once upon a blank

Long ago in a fairy tale kingdom, there was a rabbit prince.
Fill in the blanks in this four-page comic to complete his story.

What are they saying?

Give the characters names.

Once upon a time there was a rabbit prince.

Ahem, you mean a HANDSOME rabbit prince named Hank.

He lived in a castle with his best friend Pete.

Hello, again Pete

Hello hank

One day, they were invited to the fairy king's ball. The rabbit prince had a coach, but nothing to pull it. His fairy godmother came to the rescue.

Here, this creature will pull you there in no time!

Thank you, fairy godmother!

I've never seen a beast like THAT before.

Draw a magical creature to pull the carriage.

What are the guests at the ball saying and thinking?

Is the fairy king welcoming his guests? Or complaining about the food?

What's on the fairy queen's mind? Is she enjoying herself?

Wha- are the dancing mice talking about?

Write a sound effect for a noise of something scary that's coming to get them.

Try saving up surprises for after a page turn. For example, on this page, there's suddenly a great big... well, that's for you to decide.

Draw what the characters are running away from and add sound effects for the noise it's making.

Just then, the fairy godmother appeared.

Don't worry, boys, I'll save you with one of my spells.

Alacka Dabra

SAPP

What sound does the spell make?

She's turned it into a

Pig

BYEEE!

Draw what the fairy godmother has turned the scary thing from the opposite page into.

Thankia

...and they all lived happily ever after. THE END.

Plotting

A comic needs a plot — or story — with a beginning, a middle and an end. Here's one way to create a plot.

Now try writing some notes for a plot of your own.

Your story's title: Bleg

Fill in the blanks to create your plot.

Beginning

Your main character is...
(Who? What?) Bleg

Weird

Your story starts in...
(Place) Big house

The story gets started when... year 1652

Middle

One problem your character comes up against is...

This is too exciting. I can't bear to look.

Your character reacts by...

There's a surprise when...

End

The character's problems are solved when...

At the end of the comic, your character is....
(Feeling? Doing?)

My story had a happy ending... but yours doesn't have to.

Rough planning

scribble!

Once you've decided what happens in your comic, decide how many panels you want to use to tell the story. It can be helpful to write a list and sketch out a small, rough version showing what will happen in each panel.

PANEL 1: A knight is riding. A king calls to him for help.

PANEL 2: On the castle roof, the king points out a dragon.

PANEL: 3 The knight fights the dragon with his lance.

PANEL 4: The dragon's fire melts the lance.

PANEL 5: The knight pushes the dragon into the river.

PANEL 6: The dragon gives up. Without its fire, it has no power.

Mini, rough comics like this are often called thumbnails.

Try drawing your own rough sketches for a comic — perhaps the story you planned on page 25. The sketches can be as messy as you like, and you don't have to use all the panels. Start by jotting down a list on rough paper of what you want to show in each panel.

Title: B leg.

Pencils and inks

It's often a good idea to draw your comics in pencil first, then pen. The first half of this comic shows the stages many comic book creators go through.

Pictures and speech bubbles drawn in pencil

Black ink added over pencils

Pencil lines erased

Foreground (the front of the picture) filled in

Background filled in and shading added

Black ink added over the words in speech bubbles

Go over the rest of this strip in black pen. Then fill in the
foreground and background in pencils or pens.

Your own comics

Now it's over to you. Fill the rest of the book with your own comics. Add the titles of your comics here as you go along.

BLEG

(Mix and match comic, pages 33-37)

(Good day, bad day, pages 39-43)

(Superheroes vs robots, pages 46-49)

(Dinos in danger, pages 52-55)

(Pirates and treasure, pages 58-61)

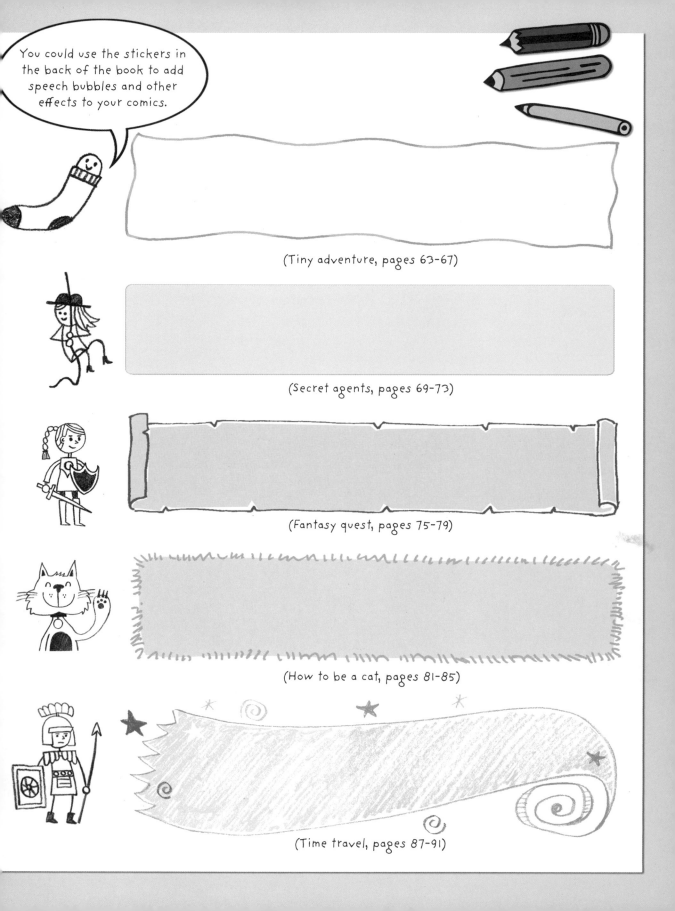

You could use the stickers in the back of the book to add speech bubbles and other effects to your comics.

(Tiny adventure, pages 63-67)

(Secret agents, pages 69-73)

(Fantasy quest, pages 75-79)

(How to be a cat, pages 81-85)

(Time travel, pages 87-91)

Mix and match comic

Choose from these characters and places to create a comic. There are suggestions for events and hints along the way to help you.

Characters

Astronaut on the run from the space police

Pirate mermaid

Bear who's obsessed with watching TV

Excitable robot

Talking skull with a bad attitude

Queen bee

Grumpy circus performer

Mysterious woman on horseback

Annoying little brother or sister

Places

An underground city

Magical library

An alien planet

A park

A supermarket

A spooky forest full of eyes

Fairyland

Ancient Egypt

Now start your comic. ➡

Continued ➡

A new character arrives. Pick one from the page opposite.
What do the two characters say to one another?

What's your title?

Pick a main character and a place for your story to start.

Show your character going about her or his daily life. You could divide up the panels if you like.

Drawing conversations

Single speaker

Speaker and listener

Two speakers. The first speaker's bubble is higher than the second speaker's.

33

Things take a turn for the worse. Pick an event that makes things more difficult for the characters.

Events

A character...

...gets kidnapped.
...is sucked through a portal into another dimension.
...goes to a new school.
...goes on a journey.
...learns to fly.
...meets her or his worst enemy.
...eats or drinks something forbidden.
...flies through an asteroid field.
...climbs a mysterious flight of stairs.
...fights a duel.

Your main character finds an object that helps to make things better.

Objects

Key   Crown   Kitten   Ray gun   Rotten banana   Magic potion   Letter   Screwdriver

How do your characters react to the new place?

Screaming   Blushing   Dizzy   Excited   Falling asleep

Something unexpected happens.
(Pick another event.)

Using a huge panel can make a dramatic event seem even more
important. You can also show lots of action happening at once.

Good day, bad day

Start your comic on the next page.

Superheroes vs robots

In a superhero story, the bad guys have to be extra-powerful, or it would be too easy for your hero to beat them.

For example...

DESTROY!

CRUSH!

ARGH!

Quick! Make up a superhero to save our city.

Hurry, or there won't be any city left!

Your mission: to create a comic about a superhero who saves a city from killer robots.

Superpower ideas

I can fly you to safety.

My laser eyes can cut through anything.

Streeeetch!

Trapped under a car? No problem.

Hmm, I wonder if I could lift a whole giant killer robot?

Give your superhero a weakness too — perhaps there's something your character is super-allergic to or afraid of.

Before you start...

What's your hero like? Fill in this card.

NAME _Musch Man_

POWERS _Super super_

Strong.

WEAKNESSES _Think's hes so hands_

PERSONALITY _____

Draw your superhero here.

Create a superhero costume that matches your character's name and personality. I'm Shadow Tabby, by the way.

Cat mask

Cat logo

Boots with stripes like a tabby cat

You could include some of these things in your costume design.

Mask

Cape

Boots and gloves

Superhero logo

Start your comic on the next page.

Step-by-step killer robot

You could add different details, such as an evil logo.

Draw some killer robots rampaging through a city. Then draw your hero arriving in the next panel.

In this big panel, show how your superhero attacks the robots.

You can make your characters look as though they're moving by using lines like these.

What's your title?

Flying   WHOOSH!

Punching   SMACK!

Running super-fast   ZOOOM!

Falling   Aaaaaaaa!

Continued →

Does anyone come to help your superhero?

Mayor of Metrotown

WOO-WOO-WOO!!

Innocent bystander

Sidekick

Giant killer robots don't make themselves... who do you think is in control of these metal menaces?

Evil alien lord?

Fiendish scientist?

A mysterious supervillain?

Show your hero facing his or her enemy. What does the villain want?

Revenge?

MWAHAHA!

To take over the world?

To shrink superheroes

How does your hero defeat the evil villain and the killer robots?

BZZZZZZZT! DIE, PUNY FLESH THING!

KAPOW!

KLUNK!

The end.

How does your superhero feel at the end? Was this an average day or your hero's greatest challenge yet?

You're going to supervillain jail!

SLAM!

Wow, I'm SUPER tired!

Dinos in danger

The land of the dinosaurs is full of deadly perils... which is bad for the dinosaurs, but good for your imagination.

Flaming meteors

I'm glad I'm not a dinosaur!

Carnivorous dinosaurs

Erupting volcanoes

Make up some dinosaur characters and put them in danger.

Help meee!

Nooooo!

DANGER

Here are some ideas for dinosaurs you could use in your comic. What are their personalities like?

I could be a vicious killer.

But then again, maybe I'm just a great big teddy bear with tiny arms.

Am I cheerful? Nervous? Brave? Talkative? Really, really annoying?

Everyone can see that I'm enormous, but am I good or evil? Brainy or a little slow?

I'm a prehistoric wasp!

BZZZZ!

Am I helpful or harmful? Friend or foe?

Do your dinosaurs work as a team? Do they all like one another? Are some enemies?

50

Drawing dinos

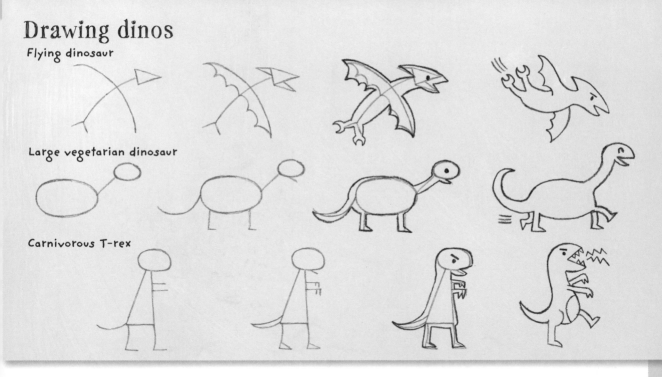

Flying dinosaur

Large vegetarian dinosaur

Carnivorous T-rex

Draw your dino character here in an action pose.

Name: James

Personality: ....

....

Try drawing a large dinosaur from below to make it look even bigger.

Shadow of a big dinosaur

Make a tiny dinosaur appear even smaller by drawing it from above.

Start your dino comic on the next page. ➡

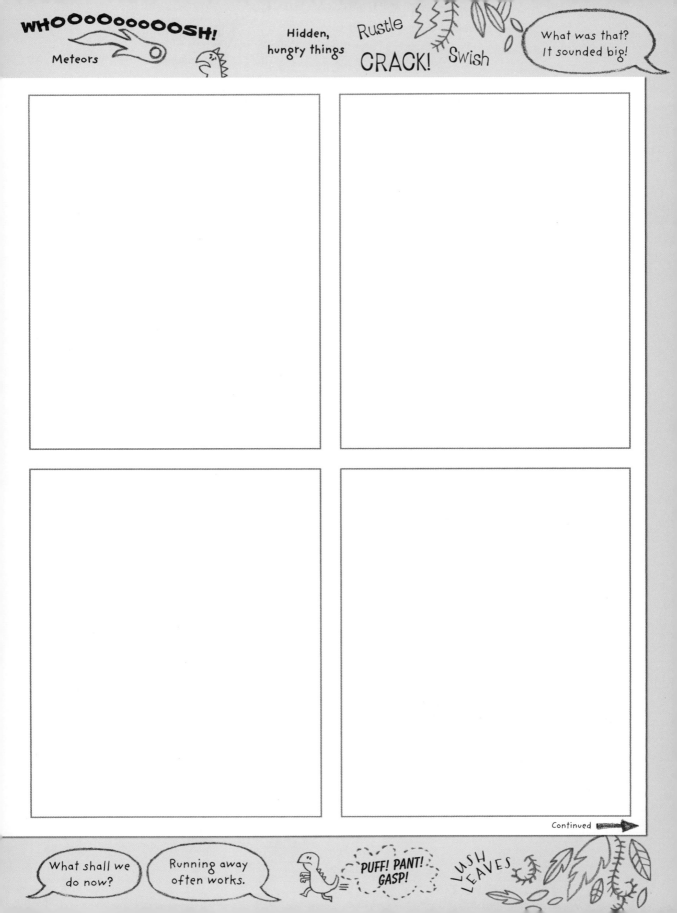

Continued ➔

Well, I've never seen one of THOSE before.

What do the dinos do now? Where do they go?

THICK FOREST · STEAMING SWAMP

Let's explore over there. It smells interesting.

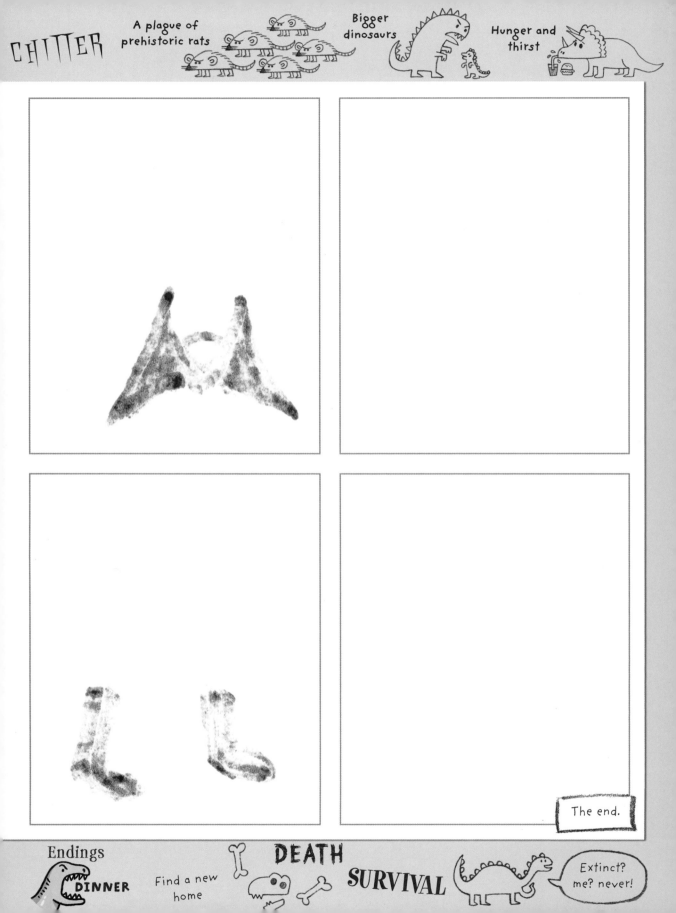

The end.

Pirates and treasure

Ahoy there, matey. It be time to make a pirate comic.

Ingredients for a pirate comic: first, a treasure map. Pirates love treasure maps.

You're so beautiful.

Then, stir in a ship full of pirates. Add stormy seas, battles and treasure islands. Season with sea monsters.

Garnish with even more pirates. Arrrrr!

Design a pirate

Add a face, hands (or tentacles) and legs (or perhaps a tail) to create your own pirate character.

Is your pirate the captain of a ship? A cabin boy or girl? The ship's cook? A sea monster?

Step-by-step pirate ship

What is your pirate ship's name?

....

Think up some places your pirates could sail to and add them to this map.

Add an X to mark the spot where the treasure is buried.

Treasure island

Mermaid cove

The sea of lost souls

Add some dangers they might face along the way.

Sharks

Sharp rocks

Terrible storms

Sea monsters

Ghostly pirate ships

Start your pirate comic on the next page. ➡

What's your title?

Where does your pirate set sail from?

Who's your pirate's crew? Here are some ideas for pirates.

Timmy Tinybones

Captain Plankwalk

Mad Lizzie Tarsniff

Where Treasure?

There's a pirate ship

heres the crew.

capiton crab

Events

58

Man overboard!

EATEN

Sea battle with enemy pirates

ATTACK!

Stock up on supplies

Continued ➡

The end.

Endings :

Huge pirate fight

Swim to safety

Sail home

Retire to a desert island

Share the loot fairly

Tiny adventure

Imagine waking up one morning to find you'd shrunk. A lot.

Eep!

thumb

To a tiny person, the world would seem like a completely different — and more dangerous — place.

A simple walk in the park would become a perilous jungle trek.

That bee's as big as a dog! And that snail's as big as I am!

What would you do? Where would you go? How would you survive?

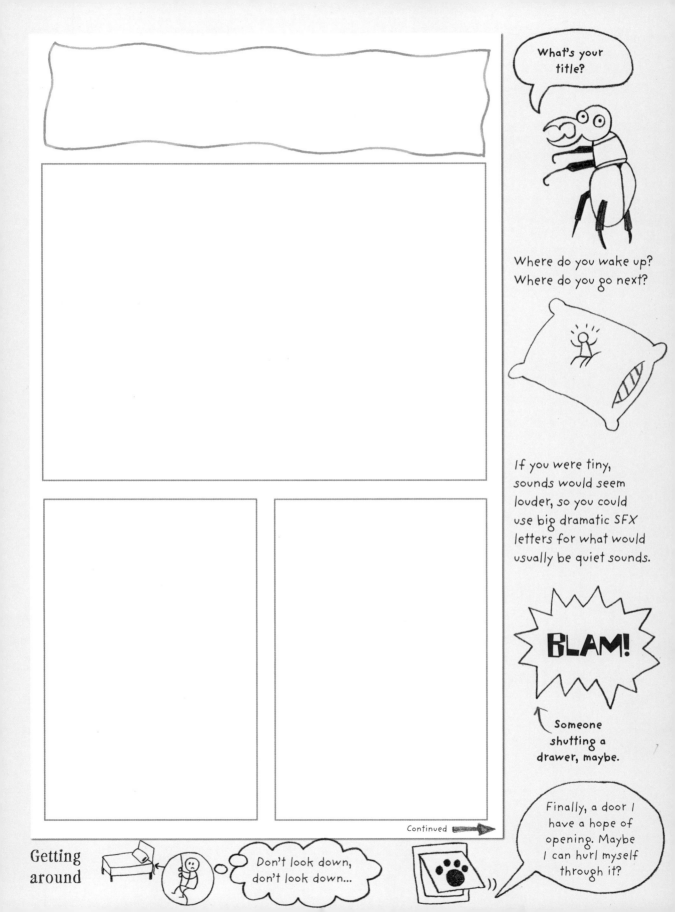

What's your title?

Where do you wake up? Where do you go next?

If you were tiny, sounds would seem louder, so you could use big dramatic SFX letters for what would usually be quiet sounds.

BLAM!

↖ Someone shutting a drawer, maybe.

Finally, a door I have a hope of opening. Maybe I can hurl myself through it?

Continued ⇒

Getting around

Don't look down, don't look down...

Physical activities

When you're tiny, you have to improvise...   Bed   Hat (made from an acorn)   Cup

Continued ➡

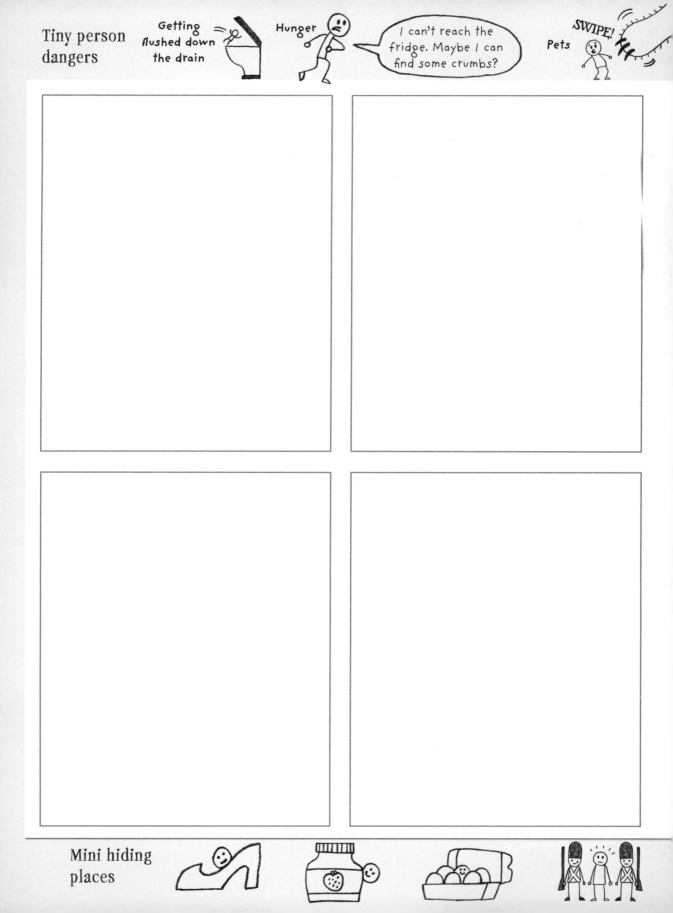

Tiny person dangers

Getting flushed down the drain

Hunger

I can't reach the fridge. Maybe I can find some crumbs?

Pets

SWIPE!

Mini hiding places

The end.

Ending ideas

You become ruler of the insects in the park.

You make a snug home in your sock drawer.

You go back to normal and write a comic about your experiences.

Secret agents

Spies operate in a mysterious, shadowy world.

Welcome, agent. I've been expecting you.

They follow secret orders.

Your next mission is to ███████ and ███████ in ██████.

Spies have to face terrifying dangers.

Give me the code or I'll let go!

But on the plus side, they do get to play with fun gadgets.

ERK!

Activate jet pack. Byeeee!

Fill in this top secret ID card for your spy character.

Is this a government agency such as MI6 or the CIA? A private company? Aliens?

?

Real name....Dylan....

Cover identity....The Villan....

Employer....Agent Grandpa....

Current mission....Stop Villan....

....From destroying the world....

CLASSIFIED

Start your spy comic on the next page. ➡

SUPER SPY

BURN AFTER READING

Flick

Mission ideas

Retrieve a top secret computer file from an enemy base.

Rescue a hostage.

Stop a bomb from going off.

This could be your spy's first mission. Perhaps it's a test to see if she or he will make a good spy?

Continued ➤

You could just draw a speech bubble against a black background for a panel in darkness.

To show a speaker without revealing her or his identity, try this.

You could draw some panels from the character's point of view, as though looking through their eyes... or their binoculars.

Gadgets and kit

 Bug (for listening in to conversations)

  Parachute

Disguise

 Fake passport

Robot surveillance bee

Handler
(a spy's
boss)

Tailing (following
enemies)

cryptography
(code making and breaking)

Biological weapon

Password

Continued ▬▶

Spy places

Top secret
headquarters

Park (a good spy
meeting spot)

Dark
abandoned
garage

AUTO DESTRUCT
MODE INITIATED...

IT'S GONNA
BLOW!

PUFF
PANT

DANGLE

The end.

Fantasy quest

When a hero goes on a journey to seek something important, it is often called a quest.

I seek the enchanted Pants of Asgaroth!

During quests, heroes face obstacles that they must overcome. Obstacles such as this big spiny monster, for example.

The Pants are mine, puny child!

Correction. They WERE yours.

Some fantasy characters you could use

Genie from a magic lamp

Wise old man

Orphaned goblin

SNIFF!

SOB!

Will you be my friend?

Tough unicorn

I will help you fight your enemies.

Evil overlord

MWAHAHAHA!

Sea serpent

Brave dwarf

Weird monster

What is your title, mortal?

Who or what is your questing hero and what is she or he seeking?

Goblin

Human

Dwarf

Sea serpent (Who says sea serpents can't be heroes?)

Quest objects

Magic shield that makes you super-strong

Fountain of eternal youth

Sacred chalice of the gods

Continued ➡

What terrible and wonderful places does your hero travel through?

Sand dunes

scorch!

SWELTER!

Forces of darkness

Fiery dragon

I eat heroes for breakfast!

Angry troll

You shall not pass!

Is it safe to go in here?

Rushing river

Snowy mountains

Deep, dark caves

Tangled forest

Continued ➡

SNARL!

Giant, poisonous spider

SSSSSSSSSSSS!

Goblin king

Off with their heads! I could use a snack.

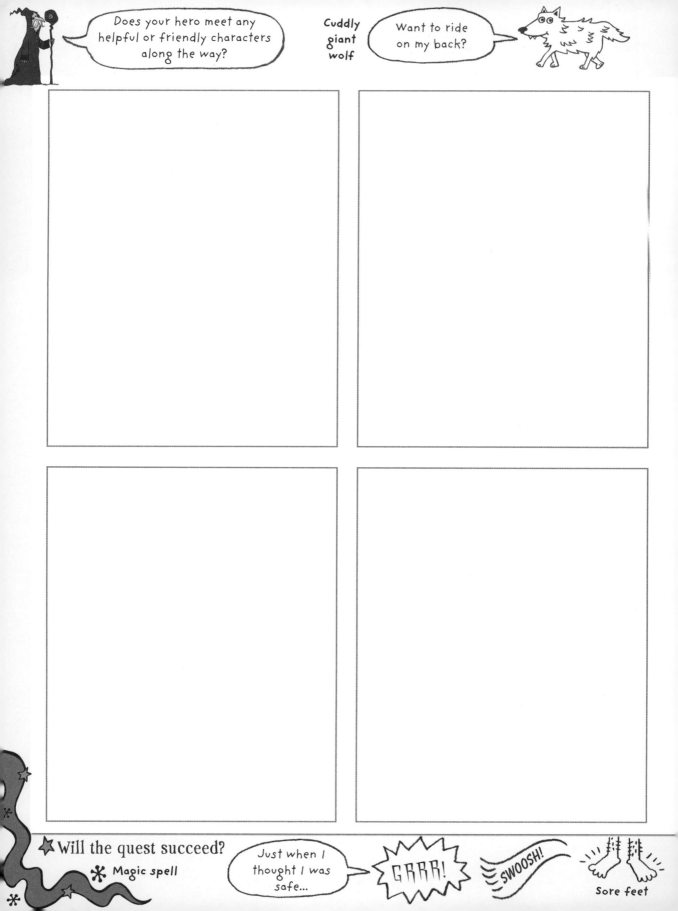

Does your hero meet any helpful or friendly characters along the way?

Cuddly giant wolf

Want to ride on my back?

Will the quest succeed?

Magic spell

Just when I thought I was safe...

GRRR!

SWOOSH!

Sore feet

How to be a cat

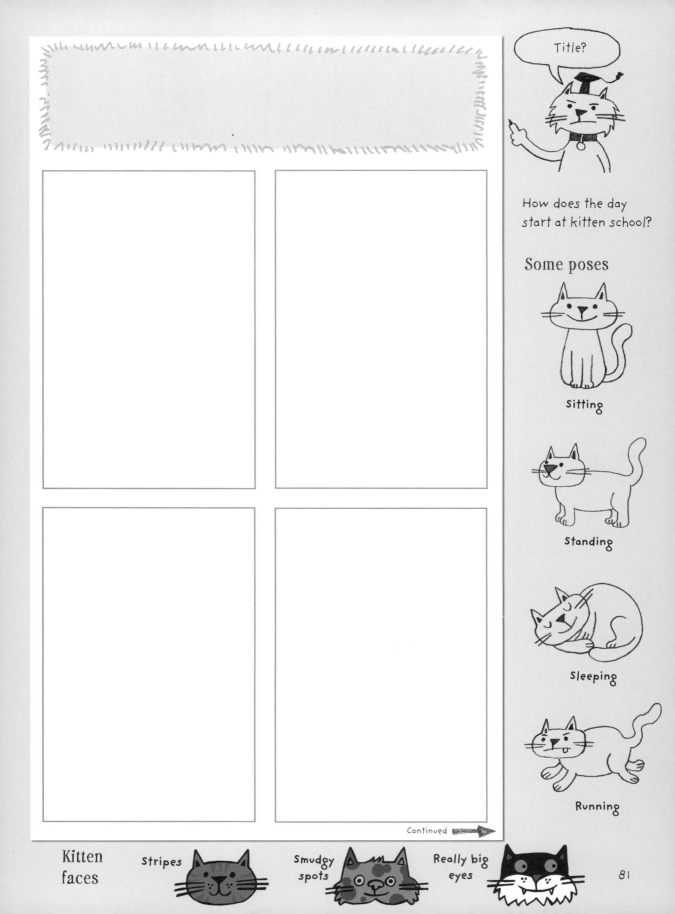

Title?

How does the day start at kitten school?

Some poses

Sitting

Standing

Sleeping

Running

Continued →

Kitten faces

Stripes

Smudgy spots

Really big eyes

What are the classrooms like at kitten school?
Do they have any classes outdoors?

Panel ideas

What's the best way to kill a mouse?

To show the teacher talking to the class, you could draw it like this.

Good afternoon Ms. Clawface.

To draw lots of kitties talking together, try this.

SIT DOWN!

If the teacher gets angry and shouts, you could write his or her speech in big letters.

What might make a cat teacher angry?

Steam

Watching videos of humans on Mewtube in class

Not sharing your toys

Claiming the dog ate your homework

What experiments might kittens do in a science class?
What songs would they sing in kitten choir?

YOWL!

Continued ➡

What might
make a cat
teacher happy?

A++

Getting the top grade
in a Pouncing exam

Putting your paw up before
you meow

A present for
teacher

How does the school day end?
What do the kittens do for fun after school?

The end.

SCRATCH! MEEP! PURRRRRRRR!

Time travel

Continued ➡

Do your characters get into any trouble?
How is life different in the past or future?

Perhaps something goes wrong... your explorers make a mistake, or the time machine breaks?

Time travel trouble   Old-fashioned diseases   Finding yourself in the middle of a brutal war   Time machine breakdown

Drawing covers

The cover of a comic has to grab your reader's attention and show what the story is about.

Here are a few covers for different types of stories.

The title is usually nice and big — easy to read from a distance.

The title could go on more than one line.

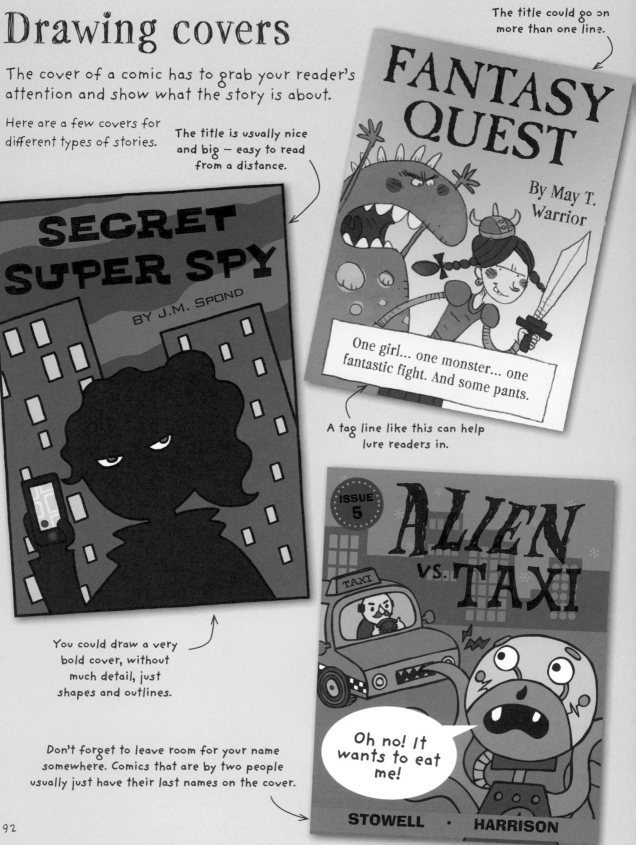

A tag line like this can help lure readers in.

You could draw a very bold cover, without much detail, just shapes and outlines.

Don't forget to leave room for your name somewhere. Comics that are by two people usually just have their last names on the cover.

Draw a cover for one of the comics you've made in this book — or for a comic that you'd love to write one day.

A few last tips

The more comic strips you write and draw, the better you get. So make comics whenever you can.

THE WORLD HAS NEVER SEEN SUCH BRILLIANCE.

AMAZING
BETTER
GOOD
OK

SCRIBBLE

Draw people and objects you see when you're out and about.

SKETCH SKETCH

Keep a book of doodles and random ideas...

...you never know when you might accidentally create a character.

I'm Mr. Stinky the Dung Beetle.

Try making collage comics.

Collage using scrap paper

Drawn-on face and other details

Try silent comics...

The pictures can tell a story on their own, without any words.

Who did what in this book?

The amazing art is by...

Jess Bradley

Neill Cameron

Freya Harrison

Laura Howell

Adam Larkum

Igor Sinkovec

You

Words by me.

Louie Stowell

Edited by me.

Ruth Brocklehurst

Designed by me.

Russell Punter

Our expert comics and literacy consultants were...

Dr. Matt Finch

Dr. Kerenza Ghosh

Usborne Quicklinks

For links to websites to find out more about writing and drawing comic strips, go to www.usborne.com/quicklinks and type in the title of this book. Please read our internet safety guidelines at the Usborne Quicklinks website.

First published in 2014 by Usborne Publishing Ltd., Usborne House, 83-85 Saffron Hill, London EC1N 8RT, England. www.usborne.com Copyright © 2014 Usborne Publishing Ltd.

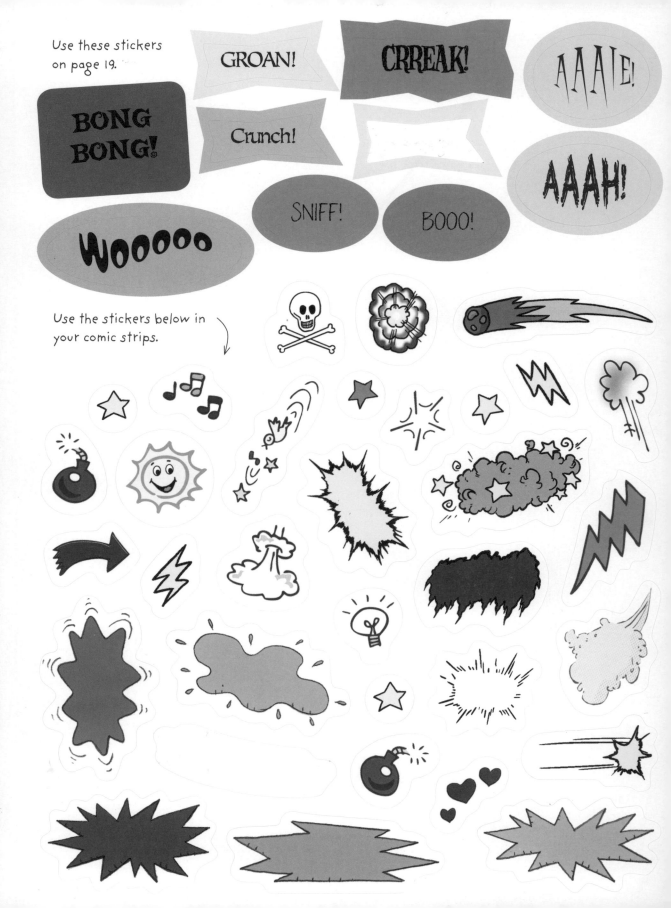

Use these stickers on page 19.

Use the stickers below in your comic strips.

Write in your own words and add these stickers to your comics.

Write in your own words and add these stickers to your comics.

Write in your own words and add these stickers to your comics.